The Snow Lambs

Debi Gliori

Hippo

For my good friends,
Johnnie, Mary, Rosie and Sam

Look out for
A Lion at Bedtime
also by Debi Gliori

Scholastic Children's Books,
Commonwealth House, 1-19 New Oxford Street,
London WC1A 1NU, UK
a division of Scholastic Ltd
London ~ New York ~ Toronto ~ Sydney ~ Auckland

First published in hardback by Scholastic Ltd, 1995
This edition published by Hippo, an imprint of Scholastic Ltd, 1997

Text and illustrations copyright © Debi Gliori, 1995

All rights reserved

ISBN: 0 590 19548 4

Printed and bound in Hong Kong

2 4 6 8 10 9 7 5 3 1

The right of Debi Gliori to be identified as the author and illustrator of this work has been asserted by her
in accordance with the Copyright, Designs and Patents Act, 1988.

It was just before teatime when the snow started falling. Sam, his dad and Bess the sheepdog were counting in the sheep from the river field.

"I think you counted that sheep twice, Dad," said Sam.
Dad was looking up at the sky where storm clouds gathered.
The branches on the old elm creaked and Sam shivered.
He looked around. I wonder where Bess is, he thought.
"If the wind gets up, that old elm could blow down across
the power lines, and we'd be in trouble," said Dad.

The wind felt full of sharp little teeth, nibbling at Sam's nose and biting his ears.

"Come on, Sam, let's get these sheep in," said Dad.

"I can't see Bess anywhere," said Sam. "Where is she?"

When the sheep were safe inside, Dad yelled, "BESS! BESS, COME HERE!"

His voice was lost in the wind.
"Come on, Sam, let's get you inside —
you look half-frozen," he said.

They took off their boots and coats in the porch. Dad bolted the door behind them.

"But how will Bess get in?" asked Sam.

"She won't," said Dad. "That dog is useless. Maybe being shut out will teach her a lesson."

BESS

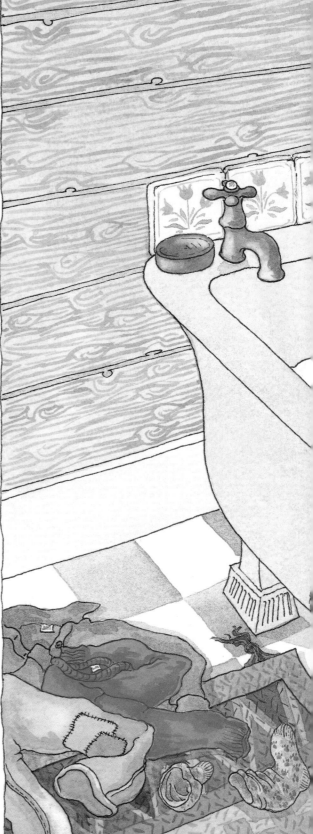

After supper it was bathtime.
As Sam jumped into his bath with a
huge SPLASH, he thought, Bess will
need a good hot bath when
she gets in.

Mum wrapped Sam up in the cocoon
of a warm towel, then dried his hair.
  "That's quite a storm brewing out
there," said Mum.
  "Will Bess be blown away?" asked Sam.
  "Don't worry, Sam. Bess can look
after herself," replied Mum.

I hope Bess doesn't have to dig her way home,
thought Sam, digging out his pyjamas.

Sam wriggled into his pyjamas.
HELP! he thought, I can't see a thing.
   Outside, snow filled the sky with
blinding white flakes.
   I hope Bess can see to find her way
home, thought Sam.

Sam asked Dad to read him a monster story, and then wished he hadn't. It was a very scary story. Outside, the wind howled. "I hope Bess isn't scared too," whispered Sam.

The wind grew louder, hurling itself at the house as if it wanted to tear the roof off.

"Bed's the safest place on a night like this," said Dad.

"No!" said Sam.

"Come on, Sam. Upstairs," said Mum.

"I'm not going," cried Sam.
"I've got to wait up for Bess."

"It's all right, Sam," said Mum. "It's only a power cut."

"I knew it," said Dad. "That old elm has brought down the power lines!"

"Oh, poor Bess!" said Sam. "How will she find our house when there are no lights?"

"Never mind her. *You'd* better find *your* way to bed!" said Dad.

But Sam couldn't sleep.
He kept thinking about Bess.

He could hear something outside,
over the howl of the wind.

It sounded like a sheep bleating.
Sam tiptoed downstairs

and unbolted the door.
At first Sam could see nothing
through the whirling snowflakes.

Then something large and wet blundered past him, followed by Bess ... BESS!

"You're covering me in mud, Bess!" laughed Sam. Then he looked round and thought, Uh, oh... And he rushed upstairs to get Mum and Dad.

"Well, Bess, it looks like you're a better shepherd than I am," said Dad. "What a clever dog to bring my best ewe home to lamb!"

Sam wrapped his arms tightly round Bess and whispered in her ear, "Brave Bess, I knew what a clever dog you were all along. I'm so glad you're home."

And later, when the wind had dropped from a howl to a whisper, the kitchen filled with newborn bleating.

"They're snow lambs!" said Sam. It was the perfect place to be born.